Bonnie Larkin Nims

Where Is the Bear in the City?

pictures by Madelaine Gill

Albert Whitman and Company
Morton Grove, Illinois

Also by Bonnie Nims

Where Is the Bear?
Where Is the Bear at School?

Published in 1992 by Albert Whitman & Company,
6340 Oakton, Morton Grove, Illinois 60053-2723.
Published simultaneously in Canada by
General Publishing, Limited, Toronto.

Library of Congress Cataloging-in-Publication Data
Nims, Bonnie Larkin.
Where is the bear in the city? / Bonnie Larkin Nims ;
illustrated by Madelaine Gill.
p. cm.
Summary: The reader may try to find Bear in the illustrations as he takes part
in many aspects of city life, including playing baseball,
getting on the subway, and observing the city from a tall building.
ISBN 0-8075-8937-3
[1. Bears–Fiction. 2. City and town life–Fiction. 3. Stories in rhyme.
4. Picture puzzles.] I. Gill, Madelaine, ill. II. Title.
PZ8.3.N6Wj 1992
[E]–dc20
92-3390
CIP
AC

4382

For my friends, the students and teachers at the
Robert E. Byrd Community Academy in Chicago.
B.L.N.

For Holly, who has lived the longest time in the city.
M.G.

The bear's on his way to the city.
I don't know where he will be,
but together we're sure to find him
if you come along with me.

I see buildings as tall as giants,
and down on the streets below,
I see cars as tiny as toys
putt-putting to and fro.

But I am looking for a bear.
Can you show me–
where is the bear?

In the midst of the crowd at the airport,
I see sort of a merry-go-round,
where bags and boxes and bundles
go in circles until they are found.

But I am looking for a bear.
Can you show me—
where is the bear?

I see cars and buses just sitting
while their drivers HONK-HONK and shout.
They're locked together so tightly,
I don't think they'll ever get out!

But I am looking for a bear.
Can you show me–
where is the bear?

Here's a pretty city street
where no one's making noise,
except a woofing dog
and laughing girls and boys.

But I am looking for a bear.
Can you show me–
where is the bear?

I see picnics and pigeons,
shining grass, shady trees,
joggers, skaters and singers–
people doing whatever they please.

But I am looking for a bear.
Can you show me–
where is the bear?

In tunnels under the city,
I see trains racing this way and that,
and a man in such a big hurry,
he couldn't hold on to his hat!

But I am looking for a bear.
Can you show me–
where is the bear?

I see a great big playing field
with a tall fence all the way round.
And if that batter swats that ball,
I'll hear a great big sound!

But I am looking for a bear.
Can you show me—
where is the bear?

I see from the top of the city
a beautiful garden of light:
flower colors–red, green, and yellow–
blooming all through the night.

But I am looking for a bear.
Can you show me—
where is the bear?

Bonnie Nims is the author of six books for young readers and numerous stories, poems, and plays. Besides her writing, she currently enjoys working with children as a volunteer teacher in a Chicago public school.

About this book she says, "I am delighted to show young children the beauty and vitality and surprises of a big city, which they will discover while looking for a fun-loving bear." Bonnie and her husband, the poet John Frederick Nims, live in the heart of Chicago.

Madelaine Gill has written and illustrated *Under the Blanket* and has illustrated several other books for children, including *Where Is the Bear at School?*

The pictures in this book were influenced by her experiences in New York City, where she lives with her daughter, Gillian.

But I am looking for a bear.
Can you show me–
where is the bear?

I see a horse-drawn carriage
that a fairy-tale king and his queen
could ride in all through the city,
seeing the sights and being seen.